PROPERTY OF SCHOOL
DISTRICT NO. 75

DATE DUE		
5/18		
1/26		
TR 3		
9/9/10		

PROPERTY OF SCHOOL
DISTRICT NO. 75

Thomas's Sheep and the Spectacular Science Project

For Readers at Braceville Elementary School!

Thomas's Sheep and the Spectacular Science Project

By Steven L. Layne

Illustrated by Perry Board

PELICAN PUBLISHING COMPANY
Gretna 2004

To Grayson Matthew, the first of our much-loved flock
—Daddy

The word "Pelican" and the depiction of a pelican are trademarks
of Pelican Publishing Company, Inc., and are registered
in the U.S. Patent and Trademark Office.

Library of Congress Cataloging-in-Publication Data

Layne, Steven L.
 Thomas's sheep and the spectacular science project / by Steven L. Layne ; illustrated by Perry Board.
      p. cm.
 Summary: Determined to prove himself at his new school by creating the best science project ever, Thomas becomes so immersed in his study of the solar system that he dreams of astronaut sheep who fly a spacecraft to Mars and beyond.
  ISBN 1-58980-210-1 (hardcover : alk. paper)
 [1. Science projects—Fiction. 2. Planets—Fiction. 3. Solar system—Fiction. 4. Space flight—Fiction. 5. Sheep—Fiction. 6. Humorous stories.] I. Board, Perry, ill. II. Title.

   PZ7.L44675Tj 2004
   [Fic]—dc22

                                          2003027708

Printed in Singapore
Published by Pelican Publishing Company, Inc.
1000 Burmaster Street, Gretna, Louisiana 70053

THOMAS'S SHEEP AND THE SPECTACULAR SCIENCE PROJECT

Thomas could not sleep. His first week as a new student at Apollo Elementary School had been a complete disaster! He worried about making friends, being late, and getting all of his homework done. In fact, Thomas worried so much that he was having trouble falling asleep at night.

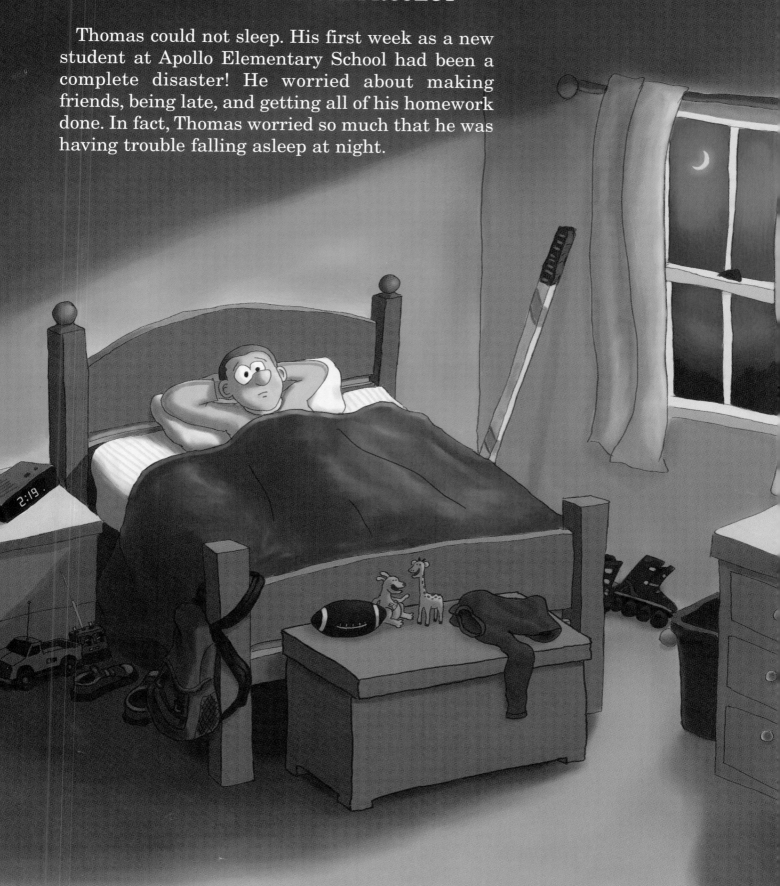

Unfortunately, he *was* getting some sleep in school—
especially when Mr. Lunar taught science.

Science class was just after lunch, and the combination
of Thomas's sleepless nights, his full stomach, and Mr.
Lunar's dry lectures put him to sleep nearly every day.

Last Friday, he had toppled his entire desk when he fell asleep during Mr. Lunar's talk on Halley's comet. Thomas had righted his desk just in time to hear Mr. Lunar's assignment. Every student had to create a science project on the solar system by next week!

In order to show everyone what kind of a student he really was, Thomas wanted to create a truly spectacular science project. And that's exactly what he set out to do!

Every day after school, Thomas went straight to his room and finished all of his homework. Then, after dinner, he read his library books on the solar system.

By the time he slipped into bed each night, something amazing would happen. Instead of worrying about school, Thomas thought about the solar system. Soon, the ideas in his books combined with his vivid imagination, and he was creating marvelous adventures starring the four zany sheep who frequently visited his dreams.

Their journey often began at space camp, where each sheep attended various training sessions. Like all astronauts, they had to prove that they were physically fit and very intelligent. Also, every sheep needed to demonstrate the ability to remain calm in uncomfortable situations.

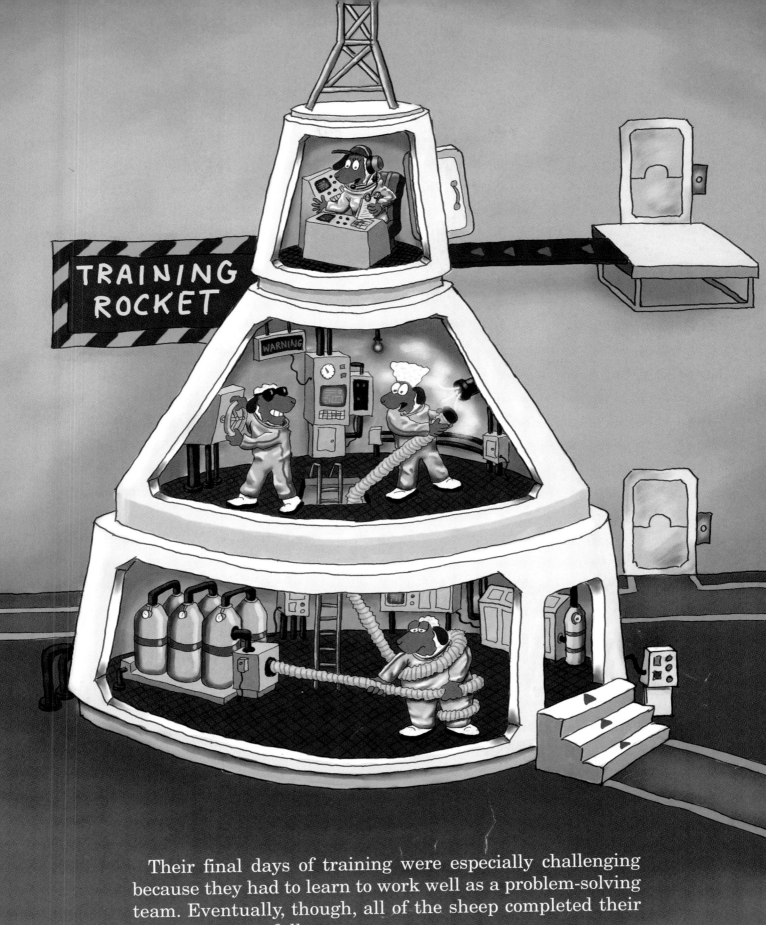

Their final days of training were especially challenging because they had to learn to work well as a problem-solving team. Eventually, though, all of the sheep completed their training successfully.

When it came time to launch, a certain sheep needed extra encouragement to board the spacecraft, but eventually, his friends persuaded him.

When they were finally all buckled in, Thomas's sheep rocketed into orbit to study the solar system.

Their first stop was Mercury. Since Mercury is so close to the sun, it was very hot during their visit. Fortunately, every sheep found an interesting way to keep cool while touring the planet.

Next, they visited Venus. The cloud cover on this planet made it the perfect place for games like hide-and-go-*sheep*. Some sheep, however, do a better job of hiding than others do.

They waved to their home planet, Earth, as they blasted past it on the way to the Red Planet—Mars.

Once there, however, the sheep could not agree on what to do. One wandered off to collect rock specimens. Two others explored a canyon that was even bigger than the Grand Canyon on Earth.

The fourth sheep spent time searching for the little green Martians he had heard about ever since he was a lamb—but, of course, he didn't find any.

Soon the sheep were maneuvering carefully through the asteroid belt that separates Mars and Jupiter. Their ship spun every which way trying to avoid the asteroids.

Unfortunately, a certain sheep became dizzy and accidentally upset the gravity controls inside the rocket!

When the sheep eventually arrived on Jupiter, the largest planet in the solar system, they each wore a bright multicolored outfit to celebrate the colorful bands of clouds that surround this planet.

They hadn't been exploring for long when they remembered that Jupiter's "Great Red Spot" is really a giant storm in the atmosphere, and they decided they had better leave. Some sheep are afraid of storms.

The sheep were very excited to inspect the famous rings around the planet Saturn; however, not all of the sheep read the rule book on ring inspection. It is important to remember, when inspecting a planet's rings, that they are not solid!

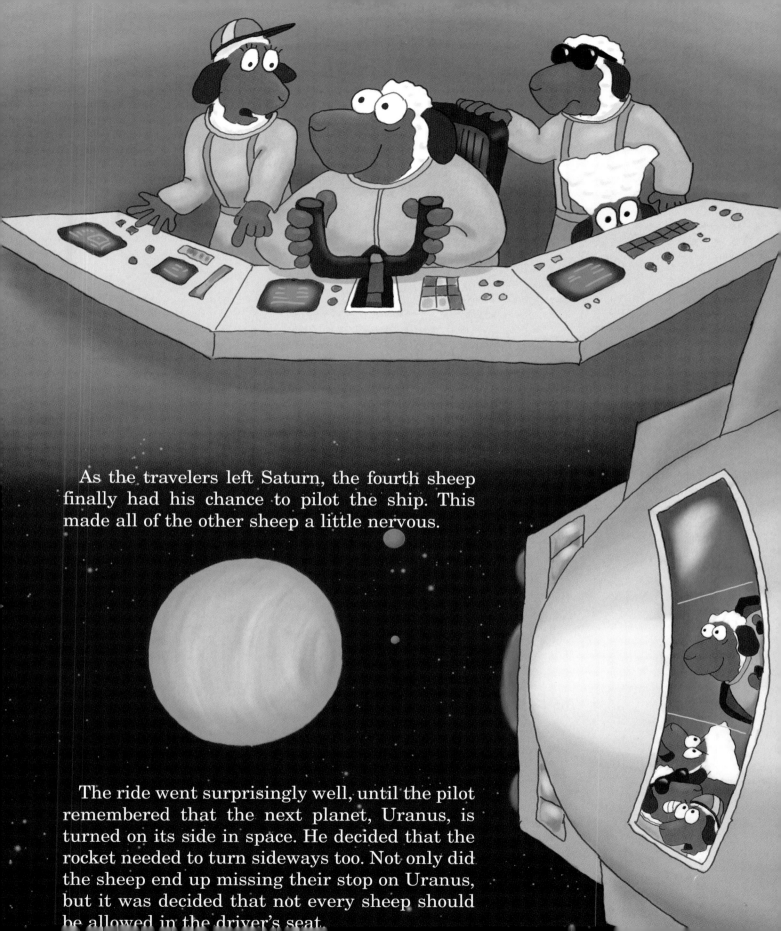

As the travelers left Saturn, the fourth sheep finally had his chance to pilot the ship. This made all of the other sheep a little nervous.

The ride went surprisingly well, until the pilot remembered that the next planet, Uranus, is turned on its side in space. He decided that the rocket needed to turn sideways too. Not only did the sheep end up missing their stop on Uranus, but it was decided that not every sheep should be allowed in the driver's seat.

They were all relieved when they landed safely on
Neptune, the planet named after the Roman god of the
sea. In honor of this planet's name, every sheep found a
way to celebrate water while on Neptune. Some had
more fun than others did.

On the way to Pluto, the sheep ran into terrible trouble. Their rocket was not staying on course, and they were heading straight for a black hole!

It seemed that a certain sheep had been eating his Puffy Cheesies near the rocket's guidance system, and the crumbs had jammed the controls. The only way to fix the rocket was for one of the sheep to go on a dangerous spacewalk. No sheep wanted to go, so they took a vote. It was *almost* unanimous.

Soon the Puffy Cheesies were locked up, and the rocket was back on course for Pluto. The sheep had already decided that since Pluto is the smallest planet in the solar system they would each leave something behind that had been special to them when they were little lambs. One sheep left a toy racing car, and another left some building blocks. A third sheep left a book that her mother used to read to her at bedtime.

The fourth sheep wanted to leave something very special, but when it actually came time to go, he had trouble giving up any of his treasures. The other three sheep had to make the decision for him.

Finally, it was time for them to reboard the rocket ship—some more reluctantly than others—and head back to the planet Earth. They had an important engagement there that they did not want to miss!

Science-project presentation day at Apollo Elementary School arrived with tremendous excitement, and only moments after the bell rang, the classroom was bursting with energetic children and fabulous science projects.

IMPACT CRATERS

FLOUR

SOLAR POWER

ORBITS

One project, though, was clearly receiving more attention than any other. To everyone's surprise, Thomas volunteered to share his project first. He hoped it would be the most spectacular science project anyone in the school, including Mr. Lunar, had ever seen. And . . .

SCIENCE PROJECTS TODAY!

it certainly was!

SURFACE ROVER
by Thomas